Mutt Dog!

Stephen Michael King

SCHOLASTIC

In the city lived a dog . . .

who belonged to no-one.

He had to be brave,

and fast,

and smart . . .

just to survive.

He ate whatever he could find.

And looked for a new place to sleep . . .

every night.

One evening he found a halfway house.

Inside there were people

who were cold

and tired . . .

like him.

There wasn't enough room . . .
or even enough food for a dog.

A lady who worked there
tried to put him outside,

but the scruffy dog
wiggled free . . .

and hid in a corner.

What am I going
to do with you?

She gave him a biscuit . . .

and made him a bed.

The next morning,
he was on his way. . .

This is no place
for a stray dog.

I wish you
could stay.

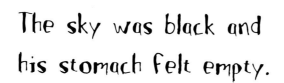

The sky was black and
his stomach felt empty.

He looked for breakfast,

and a new place to sleep.

'Wait! Scruffy dog!'
called a voice.

Would you like
to come home
with me?

It was the lady from
the halfway house.

They left the city, and the air filled with new smells.

His new family gave him the first bath he'd ever had.

They brushed out
his matted knots,

gave him food from
a big tin can . . .

and something
delicious to chew.

Everyone thought up all sorts
of names —

Bear,

Winston,

Tyrone,

Radiator,

Piccasso,

Fly,

Sigmund,

Heathcliff,

Errol,

Dingo,

Splot,

Dustin,

Affro,

Dredd!

But most of the time everyone called him . . .

Mutt Dog!

Mutt Dog
is brave,

and fast,

and smart.

He's gentle and loyal,

and each night when he goes to sleep . . .

he knows where he belongs.